W9-BYA-164

Disney

Bedtime Favorites

Disney PRESS
LOS ANGELES • NEW YORK

Contents

All illustrations by the Disney Storybook Art Team

Published by Disney Press, an imprint of Buena Vista Books, Inc.

For information address Disney Press, 1200 Grand Central Avenue, Glendale, California 91201.

Printed in the United States of America

Fourth Edition, June 2020

Library of Congress Control Number: 2019907674

10 9 8 7 6 5 4 3

ISBN 978-1-368-07121-5

FAC-038091-22213

For more Disney Press fun, visit www.disneybooks.com

Disney

Winnie the Pooh

What Good Friends Do

One night in the Hundred-Acre Wood, a nervous Piglet could not sleep.

"Oh, d-d-d-dear," Piglet said. "I better just stay here until morning, keeping watch for heffalumps, woozles, and all other creatures that come out at night!"

The next morning, Pooh knocked on Piglet's door. But there was no answer. Ever curious, Pooh opened the door and stepped inside. He found his friend shivering beneath the covers.

"Oh, bother," said Pooh. "What's the matter, Piglet?"

"Don't you hear it, Pooh?" asked Piglet.

"I do hear it," said Pooh. "And it sounds lovely to me." All Pooh could hear was the birds.

"Not the birds, Pooh," said Piglet. "It's the woozles and the heffalumps that set their traps inside my house!"

"I don't see anyone in here except you and me, Piglet," said Pooh.

"How can that be?" asked Piglet. "I'm sure they are here. Those creatures kept me up all night."

"Perhaps you were dreaming," said Pooh. "Let's look around to make sure they're not here."

"What's that whooshing and whistling?" cried Piglet.

"It's the wind blowing through your curtains," Pooh said.

"Are you sure?" asked Piglet. "It sounds rather woozle-ish to me."

"If there was a woozle about, I think I would know it," Pooh said.

Soon Rabbit stopped by with some freshly picked apples.

Just then, a horrible banging and clanging began, sending Piglet beneath a chair.

"I believe your pipes need some tightening," said Rabbit. "My tool kit and I will be back in a jiffy!"

They heard a *plip, plip, plop* throughout the kitchen. Pooh went over to Piglet's sink and turned the faucet left and right.

"That should do the trick," he said.

"I do hope Rabbit hurries," said Piglet. "All these noises are making me nervous."

Pooh turned to his friend. "I think I know a way to help, Piglet. What if you pretend to be brave, even if you're really not?"

Piglet considered this. "What good is pretending when there are heffalumps and woozles about?"

"Well," Pooh said, "perhaps you might get so busy being brave that you forget that you're pretending. And then you can go on being brave." Pooh spent the rest of the noisy day at Piglet's.

"Oh, d-d-d-dear, Pooh," said Piglet. "I'm not pretending to be brave very well, am I?"

"I'll keep watch tonight, Piglet," said Pooh, tucking Piglet into bed. "Maybe we can try pretending in the morning." But soon Piglet heard a strange sigh, followed by a long snore.

Carefully, on tippy-toes, Piglet made his way over to Pooh's chair. Sure enough, the strange sounds were coming from Pooh!

"That's funny," said Piglet. "Pooh sounds just like a woozle when he snores. But I'd better let him sleep. I'll keep watch myself."

In the morning, Pooh awoke to find Piglet outside, waving a broom in the air.

"Look, Pooh! I'm shooing these blackbirds away. They've been cawing and screeching at me."

Pooh looked at his friend. “Let’s take a walk. When you see there’s nothing scary out there, it might help you feel brave.”

Piglet stopped to admire a butterfly and then noticed he was alone. Just then, Piglet heard a strange humming sound. “Pooh,” he whispered. “Is that you?”

When there was no answer, Piglet began to shake. He quickly hid behind a thick oak tree. *“Be brave, be brave, be brave,”* Piglet said to himself again and again.

Piglet took three deep breaths. Then he stepped out from behind the tree. “Be brave,” he whispered.

Piglet walked on bravely, looking for Pooh. He listened closely when he heard a curious crunching and scrunching.

"I'm not afraid," Piglet told himself. "It's just some birds, or squirrels, or mice, or . . . Pooh! Is that you?"

"Yes, it's me, Piglet," said Pooh. "The leaves are making quite a racket today. But you didn't hide. You didn't shout or cry. You were very brave! However did you do it?"

"I'm not sure," said Piglet. "I wasn't even pretending. I just told myself that I wasn't afraid."

Pooh hugged his friend.

"I couldn't have done it without you believing in me, Pooh. That helped me believe in myself," Piglet said.

"Well," said Pooh, "that's just what good friends do."

Thumper's Nighttime Adventure

One beautiful day, Thumper was playing outside in the sunshine. As he was exploring the forest, he spotted his friend Dizzy the opossum.

"Hiya!" Thumper said. "Want to come play?"

Dizzy yawned. "That sounds fun," he said sleepily, "but I'm getting ready for a nap. Maybe next time, okay?"

"Okay," Thumper said, and he scampered away.

Thumper and Dizzy had been friends for a while, so Thumper knew the opossum napped a lot during the day. But would Dizzy really rather sleep than play?

Later, Thumper asked his papa, "Why is Dizzy always so sleepy?"

"Ahh," said Papa. "Well, he's not always sleepy. Opossums are nocturnal. That means they sleep a lot during the day. Then they are awake at night, when we bunnies are sleeping."

Papa led Thumper to a nearby cave. There, Thumper saw all the bats hanging from the ceiling of the cave. "These bats are nocturnal, too," Papa said. "Right now, they are getting ready to rest. But they spend most of the night flying outside, looking for food."

Wow, thought Thumper. *Awake all night? No wonder Dizzy is so sleepy!*

Thumper wondered what other kinds of animals were nocturnal.

Thumper and Papa hopped back home to Mama and the sisters. Thumper was excited to play with his sisters before bedtime. Maybe they could play tag or hide-and-seek. He always had so much fun with them. Thumper hoped Dizzy had fun with his own family after all the other animals went to sleep.

That evening, as the bunnies chased fireflies, Thumper thought about what his papa had said.

Soon Dizzy will be waking up! Thumper thought. *I wonder what nocturnal animals do all night?*

When Thumper and his sisters hopped home for bedtime, Thumper thought about the exciting things he might miss while he was asleep. Did the bats play tag under the stars? Did the opossum family have midnight picnics?

Before long, Thumper's sisters were sound asleep. Soon after, his mama and papa started to snore. But Thumper was still wide-awake.

Slowly, silently, Thumper hopped to the burrow entrance and poked his head out into the cool night breeze.

The moon was bright. The stars twinkled. Thumper went just outside the burrow and sniffed the air. He hopped a little farther and sniffed again. Thumper knew he shouldn't go out without his parents' permission. But he couldn't stop thinking about the nighttime fun he was missing. . . .

Thumper's curiosity soon got the best of him, and he bounded quickly down the path.

Before Thumper knew it, he had hopped all the way to the opossums' favorite tree. Dizzy was very surprised to see Thumper. "Shouldn't you be at home sleeping?" he asked.

Thumper giggled. "I came to see what other animals do at night," he said. "I've never been out this late before!"

"Well," Dizzy said, "my family is just about to eat breakfast. Do you want to join us?"

So Thumper had a late-night breakfast with the opossum family. They had the same blackberries Thumper usually ate during the day.

I guess nighttime breakfast isn't so different after all, Thumper thought.

After thanking the opossums, Thumper hopped away to find more nocturnal friends.

As Thumper walked through the darkness, he was startled by a voice. "Whooo's there?" Friend Owl asked from a nearby tree stump.

"It's Thumper!" the bunny replied. "Would you like to play?"

"Can't play. Looking for grass to fix up my nest!" the owl said. "Very busy night, you know."

Next, Thumper hopped down to the pond, where he saw some skunks. "What are you up to?" Thumper asked.

"We're off to take a bath," said one skunk.

"Some animals think that skunks stink!" said a second skunk.

"Not us!" said a third. "We take baths *every* night."

The skunks walked over to the shallow edge of the pond where Thumper and his sisters took their baths, too.

Thumper could take a bath anytime, so he waved to the skunks and kept on hopping.

On the far side of the pond, Thumper saw a mama duck and her ducklings snuggling together.

Thumper yawned. The ducks looked warm and comfy. And it was getting awfully late. . . .

Up in a tree, Thumper saw a squirrel and a chipmunk sound asleep. They seemed so peaceful and cozy.

Hmmm, thought Thumper. *They don't seem worried about missing nighttime fun.*

Thumper stood very still and listened to the sounds of the night. The crickets were chirping softly. Frogs were croaking down by the river. Now and then, wings fluttered through the darkness overhead. Thumper knew they were sounds of nighttime animals all around.

But they were also sleepy sounds.

At that moment, all Thumper wanted was to be in his burrow, snuggled up with his family.

Thumper hurried home. He hopped silently inside, expecting to find his family sleeping, just as he had left them.

Instead, his sisters rushed to meet him, squeezing him from all sides.

"Oh, Thumper!" exclaimed Daisy. "We were starting to worry!"

"Thank goodness you're back!" cried Tessie.

“Daisy is right. You could have gotten hurt,” Papa said.

“Papa was about to go out looking for you,” Mama added.

“I’m sorry,” Thumper said. He hadn’t meant to worry them. “I just wondered what it’s like to be nocturnal.”

Papa patted Thumper’s head. “I understand that you were curious. But you must promise never to go out at night without permission again.”

“I promise!” Thumper said.

Thumper's parents gave him extra chores as punishment.

As Thumper got ready for bed, he realized that doing chores was a little bit like his nocturnal adventure. He had eaten blackberries with the opossums, collected grass with Friend Owl, and visited with the very clean skunks.

"I guess I wasn't missing anything after all," he said to himself. Even though his nighttime adventure had been exciting, nothing was better than snuggling down in his warm, cozy burrow for a good night's sleep.

Enchanted Unicorn Adventure

Aurora—who was known as Briar Rose at the time—was teaching her aunts how to plant a garden. For weeks they had tended to the seeds, watered, weeded, and waited. And the buds were finally showing.

"Oh, won't they hurry up?" Merryweather said.

"It'll be worth the wait," Briar Rose said.

But Merryweather didn't like waiting. Later that night, she approached the other aunts.

"You know what would make the flowers bloom?" she whispered to Fauna. "Magic!"

"Oh, for goodness' sake," Flora muttered. She went to the cabinet where their magic wands were hidden. "No wands," she scolded. "We promised."

Everyone got ready for bed, but Briar Rose couldn't fall asleep. She'd planned a surprise for her aunts—and she thought it might be revealed that night! Under the light of the moon, something wonderful was happening.

"They're blooming!" Briar Rose cried as she dashed down the stairs and out the front door.

"But how could that be?" Fauna asked.

"The sun has already set," Flora said to Merryweather, giving her a stern look.

"It wasn't me!" Merryweather cried.

Briar Rose ran outside, with her aunts following close behind. They were all excited to see the flowers!

Sure enough, the garden was bursting with blooms. “Surprise!” Briar Rose shouted.

“Incredible,” Flora observed. “How can flowers bloom without sun? It’s almost like—*ahem*—magic.”

“Well,” Briar Rose began, “we planted special seeds: evening primrose, moonflower, and—”

“Night-blooming flowers!” Fauna interjected. “I should have known!”

Just then, a branch snapped. Briar Rose turned and couldn’t believe her eyes.

In the corner of the garden, a family of unicorns was grazing on the moonlit blooms! The baby's horn glittered. Briar Rose's eyes were glued to the magical creatures.

"Unicorns only come out at night—for fear of being seen," Flora said to Briar Rose. "They must have smelled the flowers. They eat petals."

Briar Rose plucked a few petals, then offered her cupped hand to the baby unicorn. It licked Briar Rose's hand as it ate. It tickled.

"We should let them be," Merryweather suggested.

"You can eat as much as you want," Briar Rose said softly to the unicorn family. "You're safe here."

Briar Rose and her aunts headed back to their cottage. It had been a great day, and Briar Rose was very proud of their night-blooming flowers. She couldn't wait to check on her enchanted visitors the next night.

Meanwhile, Maleficent's raven was out for a night flight. He spotted something unusual and immediately reported it back to Maleficent.

In her castle, Maleficent was not pleased.

"Unicorns? In that pesky cottage garden? We'll have to do something about that," she said. Maleficent didn't like anything out of the ordinary, and unicorns were the most extraordinary creatures of all. She would have none of it. "When I'm through, no one will be able to enjoy those flowers."

Maleficent began to form her evil plan. She knew how she could get rid of the enchanted creatures, but she would have to act fast. Her raven flew back off to the garden.

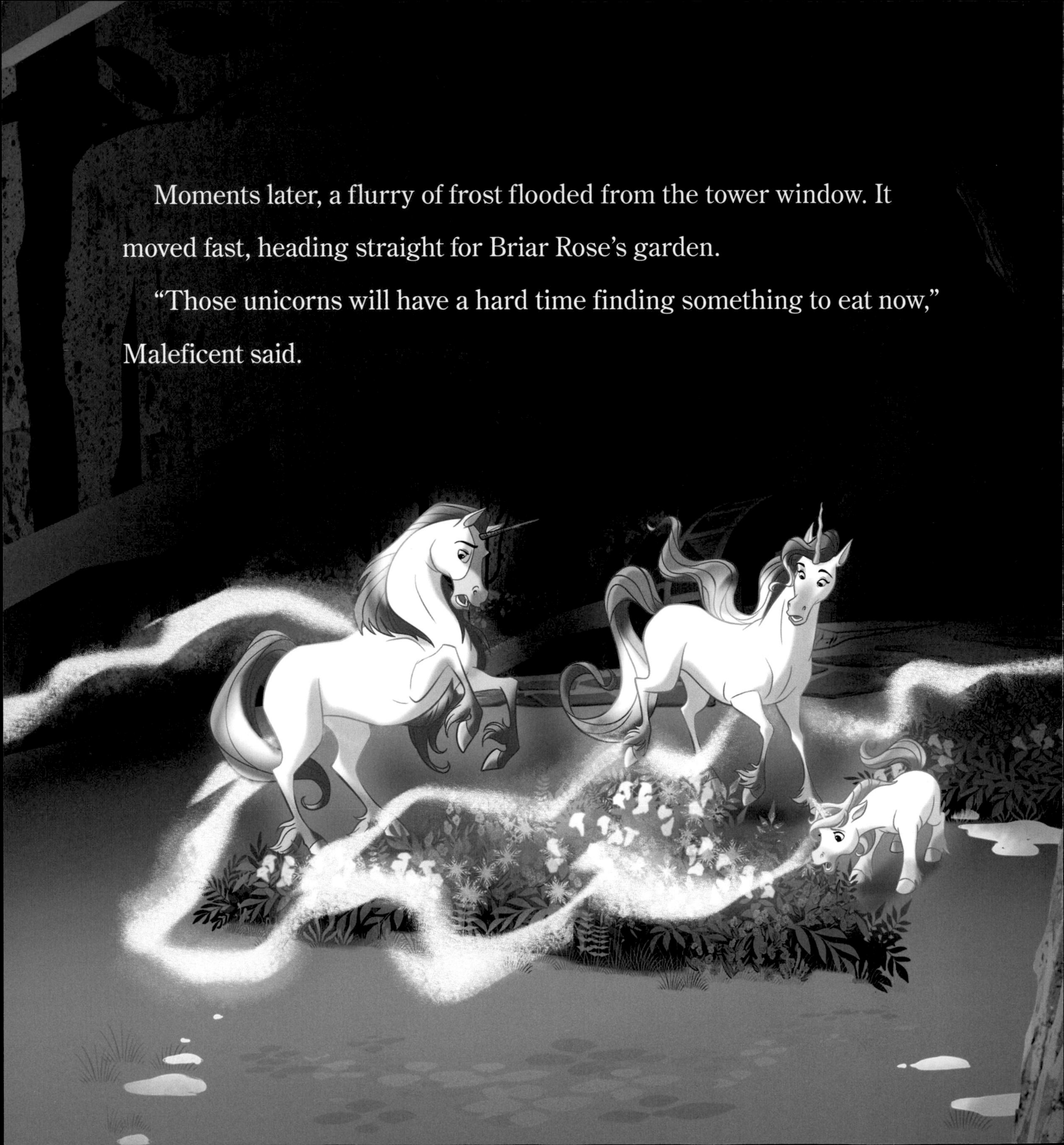

Moments later, a flurry of frost flooded from the tower window. It moved fast, heading straight for Briar Rose's garden.

"Those unicorns will have a hard time finding something to eat now," Maleficent said.

Early the next morning, Briar Rose rushed to the garden. But her excitement quickly turned to confusion. "What bad luck!" she cried. She feared her garden was ruined. Even worse—it seemed her unicorn friends were out of food.

Briar Rose had to help. She grabbed her cloak and a basket, then walked down a narrow path. *Perhaps some flowers are blooming elsewhere in the forest,* she thought. She noticed that the frost hadn't traveled far.

She walked until nightfall. Then Briar Rose caught a glimpse of a moving bush. It was the mother unicorn!

The mother unicorn had been chomping at a patch of wildflowers. “Are you trying to bring food back for the baby?” Briar Rose asked. The unicorn whinnied.

“Let me help,” Briar Rose said. And together they plucked an entire bouquet. When Briar Rose and the mother unicorn returned to the moonlit garden, Briar Rose sprinkled petals across the snow.

The next morning, Briar Rose checked on her bouquet, and to her dismay, the flowers were already wilting. Briar Rose grabbed a gardening book and flipped through the pages. "I didn't let the frost stop me then, and I won't let the wilted flowers stop me now," she said. " There are flowers that bloom even when it's cold and snowy."

"Did we plant any?" Merryweather asked.

"We did," Briar Rose answered. "Forget-me-nots. With a little help, they'll be ready by nightfall."

Briar Rose gathered her gardening tools while Merryweather roused the other aunts. They carefully watered the plants to clear and melt the snow.

Next Briar Rose instructed Fauna to prune and trim the dead leaves. Flora gathered the debris and cleared it away. By the end of the day, the garden looked good as new. And poking through the soil in the corner of the garden was a burst of flowers. The forget-me-nots had blossomed.

Just then, the baby unicorn trotted forward and sniffed the blue petals. It started eating, and Briar Rose patted the creature's head.

"I can't believe I have enchanted friends to visit with every night!" Briar Rose said.

Flora gave the other aunts a sideways glance. "My dear," she began, "as you know, flowers only last for a season."

"I'm afraid unicorns are similar," Merryweather added.

"They don't stay in one place for long," Flora said.

"But don't fret," Fauna interjected. "Maybe they'll come back again next year—"

"Just like the flowers," Briar Rose replied. As her aunts wrapped her in a warm hug, Briar Rose was certain of one thing: she could overcome any obstacle that was thrown her way—especially with the help of her family.

Detective Lucky

A **blustery wind was blowing** outside, but the Dalmatian puppies—all ninety-nine of them—were snug and cozy in their new house. The puppies crowded around Nanny, who was reading them a bedtime story.

Lucky loved bedtime stories. He especially loved ones about detectives! He wished *he* could be a detective.

When Nanny's story was over, Pongo and Perdita tucked the puppies into bed. But Lucky wasn't tired—not even a little bit! He couldn't stop thinking about all the mysteries he would solve if he were a detective.

One by one, the other puppies drifted off to sleep. Soon Lucky was the only one still awake. Suddenly, his ears twitched.

Creak, squeak, BANG!

What was that strange sound? Lucky bolted upright. Maybe this was it—the mystery he had wished for. Maybe the sound was a clue!

Lucky carefully climbed out of bed. His parents were in the living room with Roger and Anita. No one would notice if Lucky slipped through the doggy door. He could go outside, find some clues, crack the case, and be back before anyone even knew he'd left!

Lucky scampered outside. He looked around. He had never been outside alone at night. The wind had died down, but it was very dark. All around him, Lucky saw strange shadowy shapes.

Lucky thought about going back inside. But he knew that a true detective would solve his case no matter what. If he wanted to be a detective, he'd have to go on, dark or no dark.

Lucky sniffed the air. An unfamiliar smell made his nose twitch. Maybe it was another clue!

Lucky pressed his nose down to the dirt and sniffed again. There it was—the same smell! His tail wagged as he followed the scent into the woods.

This is exactly what a real detective would do! Lucky thought eagerly as he tracked the smell to a hollow log. Lucky poked his head into the log to see what was inside—and found two spooky eyes staring back at him!

Lucky yelped in surprise. He backed out of the log as quickly as he could.

Strange noises filled the air, and Lucky felt something brush by his head.

Hoo-hoo-hoo-hoo!

Flap-flap-flap-whoooooooosh!

Lucky was surrounded by spooky sounds, and he didn't know what was making any of them. And to make matters worse, he'd been so busy tracking the smell that he hadn't noticed how far he'd roamed. He had no idea where he was going or how to get home! There was only one thing to do. Run!

Lucky raced through the forest, ducking under branches and leaping over rocks. When the trees began to thin, he charged forward, running faster and faster until—*wham!* He knocked right into someone!

In a flurry of fur and tails and hisses and growls, Lucky and the stranger tumbled over and over and over. Then the puppy heard a familiar voice: "Lucky? Is that you?"

It was Sergeant Tibs, the cat who'd helped rescue Lucky and his siblings from Cruella De Vil!

"Sergeant Tibs!" Lucky cried in relief. "Help! I'm lost and I don't know how to get home!"

Sergeant Tibs knew just what to do. He led Lucky to an old barn, where the two filled in the Colonel on Lucky's situation.

"This calls for the Midnight Bark!" the Colonel said.

The Colonel lumbered over to the door and howled into the night. Lucky waited anxiously for a response. At last, it came!

Bark! Bark! Bark!

Yip! Yip-yip! Yip, yip, yip!

Arf, arf, arooooo!

The barks echoed across the countryside to the Dalmatian Plantation, where a sleepy Pongo opened his eyes.

"It's a lost pup," he whispered to Perdita. "I'll go help."

"Follow the barks. They'll lead you home again," the Colonel told Lucky. "Good luck, lad!"

"Thank you," Lucky told the Colonel and Sergeant Tibs. Then, listening closely, he ran into the night. The Colonel was right. Following the sound of the barks, Lucky soon realized he was on the way home. And now that he was less scared, Lucky was able to solve all the mysteries he'd stumbled upon—even the creaky old gate that had started it all.

Back at the Dalmatian Plantation, Pongo was shocked to see Lucky bounding up to him. "The Midnight Bark was for *you*?" he asked.

"Dad! Dad! I solved a mystery!" Lucky exclaimed. "Just like a real detective!"

"Tell me about it in the morning," Pongo whispered as he led Lucky back to bed. "And no more mysteries tonight!"

Lucky agreed and snuggled up next to his siblings, ready to fall asleep after his big adventure. Suddenly, his ears twitched.

Cro-a-a-a-a-k-squeak!

What was that strange sound?

Maybe it was a clue!

A Nighttime Stroll

"Cinderelly! Cinderelly!" Gus yelled, running into Cinderella's room. "There's a new mouse in the barn! Her name is Greta. Can she stay with us?"

Cinderella smiled at her mouse friend. "Of course!" she said. "There's always room here for one more!"

Cinderella loved her mouse friends. She had rescued them from her stepmother's cat, Lucifer, before she met the Prince. Now they lived with her in the palace.

Cinderella and the mice got to work. They wanted to make their new friend feel right at home!

The mice built a tiny bed for Greta and stuffed a mouse-sized mattress with dandelion fluff from the palace lawn. Meanwhile, Cinderella sewed Greta some new clothes, and Gus made a nightstand out of a spool of thread.

"Greta will sleep like a baby mouse!" Gus said, placing a small vase of flowers on the nightstand.

Gus couldn't wait to introduce his new friend to Cinderella!

"Greta!" Gus cried. "This is Cinderelly!"

The princess knelt to shake Greta's tiny paw with her pinkie finger. "You're very welcome here," the princess said. "You must be hungry."

Greta patted her tummy and nodded.

Cinderella smiled at her new mouse friend. "Well, why don't we get you dressed, and then we'll have a nice, filling dinner!"

While the mice had been making Greta's bed, Cinderella's bird friends had prepared a huge welcome feast. There was a baby-lettuce salad, grilled cheese and soup with tiny toast corners, and every kind of nut the palace kitchen stocked.

Greta happily dug in to the food while the mice asked her all sorts of questions. Soon Gus noticed Greta's eyelids drooping. Taking her by the paw, he showed her to her new bed.

"Oh!" Greta said, clapping in delight. "Such a snug bed! Thank you! Thank you!"

Greta climbed into her bed and was soon fast asleep, snoring softly into her dandelion pillow.

Later that night, a shadowy figure marched down a path in the royal garden.

"Halt!" one of the watchmen called. "Who goes there?"

The guard knelt down and peered into the shadowy lane. "Why, it's one of Her Highness's mouse friends!" he said.

Greta rubbed her eyes and looked around. "Where am I?" she asked, confused.

The guard smiled and told Greta that she was in the garden. Then he walked her back to the palace.

The next morning, Greta told her new friends all about her nighttime adventure. "It was so strange!" she said. "One moment I was in bed, all cozy and snug, having the nicest dream . . ."

"And then-a what happened?" Jaq asked.

"I woke up in the garden!" Greta exclaimed. "In my nightgown! With no idea how I'd gotten there!"

The mice gasped.

"I've never sleepwalked before, not ever!" Greta said, taking a bite of a blueberry.

Everyone agreed Greta's sleepwalking was likely a onetime thing. She was probably just getting used to her new bed.

"I'm sure it won't happen again," Greta agreed cheerfully.

That night, Greta went to bed confident that she'd stay put until morning. A few hours later, though, she woke up at the palace gates with no memory of how she'd gotten there!

Then, the night after that, she marched right through the gates and into the street.

"Rats," Greta said as a kind villager walked her back to the palace.

Over the next few days, Cinderella and her mouse friends did everything they could to help Greta.

Jaq tried giving her a glass of warm milk before bed. "Always helps-a me sleep tight!" he said. But that night, Greta woke up in the middle of the village.

Gus tried putting noisy crumpled paper around Greta's bed, but she marched right through it without blinking an eye.

Cinderella tried putting a mouse-sized gate at the front door, but Greta

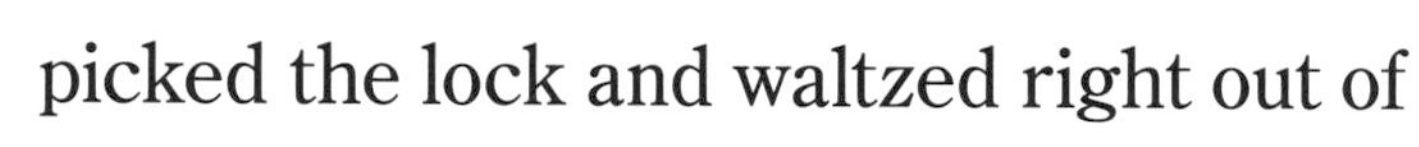

picked the lock and waltzed right out of the palace . . . without waking up!

"I didn't even know I could pick locks!" Greta said. "You learn something new every day!"

"Or every night," Gus agreed.

No matter how hard Cinderella and her friends tried to keep Greta inside the palace, nothing worked. Every night she woke up farther and farther away. Finally, early one morning, Greta woke up with sore feet in a village she didn't recognize. She'd never been that far from the palace before. She couldn't even see it on the horizon.

"Where am I?" the little mouse wondered out loud as she walked the streets. The town she'd sleepwalked into was tiny and quiet. Everyone was still asleep.

Suddenly, Greta stopped. The most glorious smell was wafting out of a little shop.

“A cheese shop!” Greta exclaimed. The glorious smell that practically had her floating closer to the door was definitely cheese. But not just any cheese.

“I’ve never smelled a cheese like that,” Greta murmured. It was stinky and rich; she was sure it would taste amazing.

"I solved the mystery!" she said, bursting through the door after she had found her way back to the palace.

Greta explained her latest adventure to her friends. "My nose has been leading me to the cheese shop every night!" she said. "It just took me a while to get there."

Everyone was curious about the amazing cheese. What could smell so wonderful that it made Greta sleepwalk all the way to the next village?

So, shortly after breakfast, Cinderella summoned the royal coach. Soon she and her mouse friends were on their way to the countryside.

"There it is!" Greta squeaked, pointing to the shop.

The coach pulled to a stop and the friends climbed out.

The humble cheese shop owner was very surprised to find himself with none other than the royal princess and a handful of mice as his first customers of the day.

It took Greta only a few seconds of sniffing around to identify the stinky cheese she'd been sleepwalking toward. "It's this one!" she said.

The shop owner happily gave Greta a sample.

"Oh, it's glorious!" Greta said. "It's like sunrise and sunset and smelly feet all rolled into one!"

Cinderella was glad her new friend had found something she enjoyed so much. With a wink at the shop owner, she bought an entire week's worth of cheese for her little friend.

That night, Greta had a wonderful bedtime snack: several tiny crackers smeared with her new favorite cheese.

"Yum!" she said. "That really hit the spot."

Then, her tummy full, she snuggled into bed—where she stayed all night.

Pepita and Dante to the Rescue!

In the little Mexican town of Santa Cecilia, the Rivera family was busy preparing for a big celebration called Día de los Muertos—the Day of the Dead. They were honoring and remembering their ancestors by making an altar called an ofrenda. It held photographs, keepsakes, and food—everything that the Rivera ancestors had loved in life. The family hung beautiful paper banners called papel picado around the room and arranged a path of marigold petals that would lead the spirits of their loved ones back home.

For nearly a year, Miguel had been filling the house with music. It was easy for him now that he had his family's approval. The music brought them all closer together.

Miguel finished singing for his mamá and his little sister, Socorro.

"Bravo, Miguel!" said Mamá. "Now, can my little músico see if Abuelita needs help in the kitchen?"

Miguel's stomach rumbled. "Sure, Mamá!" he said.

As Miguel approached the kitchen, he noticed Dante and Pepita near the door. Abuelita enjoyed having Dante around more than she once had, but she had a strict no-animal policy in the kitchen.

"Come back a little later," Miguel whispered. "Abuelita will give us tamales."

Dante wagged his tail and Pepita meowed as they left.

The kitchen was filled with the smells of scrumptious food.

"Do you need help, Abuelita?" asked Miguel.

"I'm okay, mi hijo, but eat something," Abuelita said as she continued stirring. Abuelita was making the family's favorite dishes: posole, pan de muerto, mole rojo, and much more. The food would be placed on the ofrenda as an offering for their loved ones who were no longer there.

Miguel realized something. “Abuelita, what are you making for Papá Héctor?”

Abuelita dropped her wooden spoon with a loud clatter.

“¡Ay, Dios mío! I don’t know! I didn’t even know who he was until last year!”

Suddenly, Miguel realized he needed Dante and Pepita. “I have an idea, Abuelita. Uh . . . I’ll be right back.”

Miguel rushed off to find Dante and Pepita. They were the only ones who could help him. His family had no idea that Dante and Pepita had a secret! They were creatures of the spirit realm who could travel between the Lands of the Living and the Dead. Miguel ran down the streets of Santa Cecilia.

He found Dante and Pepita taking a nap in the gazebo near Mariachi Plaza. “I need both of you. Can you help me?” Miguel asked.

Dante barked, and Pepita purred. Miguel exhaled. “Thanks, guys! Can you get Papá Héctor a message?” He handed Dante a note.

Dante wagged his tail before dashing away with Pepita.

Dante and Pepita dodged around crowds in the cemetery and ran all the way to the Marigold Bridge, which could be seen only by visiting spirits. As soon as they reached the bridge, they magically glowed as they transformed. Pepita grew from a little alley cat into a mighty flying jaguar, while Dante sprouted a pair of wings.

"Rooooo-roo-roo-roo," mumbled Dante, trying not to drop Miguel's note. He spotted a few of the dead Riveras near Marigold Grand Central Station.

The dead Riveras looked up and saw the two spirit guides overhead.

"Look, it's Pepita!" shouted Tío Felipe.

"And Dante!" said Tía Victoria.

When Dante and Pepita landed, they gave the note to Mamá Coco, who now lived in the Land of the Dead. "It's urgent," she said, reading the note. "Miguel needs to know what my papá wants for the ofrenda."

"Follow us to the plaza!" said Tía Victoria.

The plaza was filled with a giant crowd. Mamá Imelda noticed the spirit guides and stopped singing. "¿Qué pasa? Why are Dante and Pepita here?"

Mamá Coco handed the note to Papá Héctor. He was touched that Miguel was concerned about his first Día de los Muertos. After he wrote down his favorite dishes, he gave the note back to Dante.

The dead Riveras waved goodbye as Dante and Pepita soared into the sky. Pepita swooped toward the Land of the Living. Dante veered slightly off course, greeting other spirit creatures nearby. But Pepita knew they were running out of time. She grabbed Dante with her talons and placed him on her back for safekeeping.

"Rooooo-roo-roo-roo!" Dante crooned as they flew over the Marigold Bridge.

Dante and Pepita transformed back into a dog and cat when they returned to Santa Cecilia. They dashed toward the Rivera house.

Miguel gave them a big hug when they arrived. “Thank you, Dante and Pepita! You two saved the day!”

Miguel could not reveal Dante's and Pepita's secret identities. Instead, he told Abuelita that he found the list in one of Mamá Coco's journals. She took the list from Miguel and kissed his head. "¡Gracias, Miguelito! I have just enough time to make these dishes before the festivities begin."

Later that night, Papá Héctor, Mamá Imelda, Mamá Coco, and the rest of the Rivera ancestors crossed over the Marigold Bridge.

They walked through the cemetery and followed the path of marigolds that their family had left for them.

When the dead Riveras arrived at the house, they admired the ofrenda that the family had worked so hard to put together.

The whole Rivera family, both the living and the dead, enjoyed the celebration together. Even Dante and Pepita joined in on the festivities. Miguel strummed his guitar as Dante and Pepita enjoyed their well-deserved tamales.

Disney

Peter Pan

An Adventure for Wendy

Peter Pan and the Lost Boys loved listening to Wendy's bedtime stories. Tinker Bell, too, never missed a telling. They all delighted in her gripping tales of swashbuckling pirates, hidden treasures, and magical pixie dust.

But one night during story time, the Lost Boys all looked bored. Even Michael and John found their sister's tale dull.

"Please, tell us a new story," Michael said.

"Where will I find the inspiration for a fresh story?" Wendy wondered aloud. Then it came to her. Wendy's bedtime stories all starred Peter Pan. All she needed for a brand-new story was an adventure with Peter.

The next morning, Wendy bounded out of bed, ready to join Peter Pan on an exciting excursion. But Peter was nowhere to be found.

"I'm sorry, old chaps," John said, pushing up his glasses. "I saw Peter and Tink leaving extra early for their outing this morning."

"You need Peter Pan to have an adventure," declared Nibs.

"What will you do, Wendy?" asked Tootles.

It was true. Peter was always the daring hero of Wendy's stories. But Wendy wasn't concerned. "Now, boys, don't you worry," said Wendy. "I'll just have to create my own adventure."

The Lost Boys looked doubtful. But Wendy was determined. "I'll head for the sea," she said. "There's always adventure to be had there."

Wendy took a shortcut through the jungle on her way to the water. She ran under the rushing waterfall, skipped over the stepping stones, and greeted the hippopotamus that lived in the river.

Then she looked up to see an orangutan family racing between the trees. "That looks like a grand time!" exclaimed Wendy. "Finding an adventure can wait a little while longer, I'm sure."

So Wendy joined the fun up above. She and the orangutans swung high above the ground, from tree to tree to tree.

"I wish I could spend all day with you," said Wendy when everyone stopped to rest. "But I'm in search of an adventure." She would not let the Lost Boys down.

Wendy said goodbye to her new friends, then headed toward the bluffs that met the sea.

As Wendy skipped past the shimmering Mermaid Lagoon, she heard someone cry out, “Help!”

"Oh, dear!" gasped Wendy. A mermaid was stuck in a fishing net. Her friends were nowhere to be seen. Finding a bedtime story would have to wait once again. Wendy dove into the water, swam toward the mermaid, and rescued her from the net.

"Thank you for saving me," gushed the mermaid. "You're so brave. Won't you stay and play in the lagoon for a while?"

Wendy and the mermaid splashed and laughed in the water. "This is so much fun," cried Wendy as she came up from a dip in the cove. "But I really must be going. I still have to find my adventure."

She left her mermaid friend and went off in search of her bedtime story.

Wendy hiked along the coast, past Blind Man's Bluff, heading toward a rowboat moored at the dock. Once she reached the boat, Wendy thought she could finally start her adventure. Then she'd have a bedtime story to tell.

But when Wendy arrived at the rowboat, she found Smee trying to steal it.

Her bedtime story would have to wait. She couldn't let Smee take the Lost Boys' boat!

"Now, Smee, you leave that boat alone," warned Wendy. "It belongs to the Lost Boys."

The pirate grinned. "You'll have to fight me for it first, little lass," he challenged.

Wendy dueled with Smee, using all the sword skills she'd learned from Peter (and a few tricks of her own). Soon victory was hers, as was the boat.

Her adventure could finally begin.

But as Wendy looked to the sky, she saw the sun was setting on the horizon. It was time to head back.

Wendy returned to the hideout feeling defeated. She'd failed to have an adventure. There would be no new bedtime story that night.

She stood outside the hideout, knowing her friends would be disappointed listening to the same old bedtime story. *There's always tomorrow,* she thought as she climbed into the hideout.

When the Lost Boys gathered around, Wendy apologized. “I’m sorry, boys. I meant to have a marvelous adventure today, but instead I swung through the trees with the orangutans, saved a mermaid, and fought off a pirate.”

The Lost Boys listened in awe. Peter Pan was enthralled. Swinging from the trees? Swimming in the lagoon? Dueling with Smee?

"Wendy, what a thrilling day you had!" Peter exclaimed.

"You're so courageous," said John.

The Lost Boys all agreed it was the best bedtime story they'd ever heard. "Hooray for Wendy!" they cheered.

Looking back on her day, Wendy realized they were right. She'd created her own adventure all by herself. What a wonderful feeling!

That night, Wendy snuggled into her warm bed, dreaming about all the big adventures she'd have the next day.

Ariel and the Ghost Lights

Late one night, Ariel woke from her dream to the sound of someone coughing.

Ariel's sister Andrina was very sick. She had woken with a fever and a scratchy sore throat.

"I'll bring you some night lily," Ariel whispered. Freshly picked night lily made a powerful medicine.

"You can't!" croaked Andrina. "Haven't you heard? The doctor hasn't been able to gather night lily for days. They say the flowers are guarded . . . by a ghost!"

Andrina flinched. Her throat hurt too much to talk.

Ariel wasn't afraid of ghost stories. Andrina needed medicine right away, and Ariel was going to get it for her.

She crept out of the palace and woke Flounder. Together, they swam toward the edge of Atlantica.

At the kingdom's border, they saw guards peering out into the dark ocean. Small blue lights moved in the distance!

"What are they looking at?" asked Flounder.

"Shhh . . . they'll hear you!" Ariel whispered.

"There they are," one guard said. "The ghost lights. They'll make you follow them, and you'll be lost forever."

"You hear that?" whispered Flounder. "Maybe we should go back." Ariel shook her head firmly. She pulled Flounder along by the fin, and they took extra care as they snuck past the guards.

The lights bobbed and danced as they got closer.

"W-w-what do you think it is?" asked Flounder.

"What does it look like, Flounder?" Ariel asked.

"Is it a sh-sh-shark?" Flounder was so nervous he could barely talk.

"Don't be such a guppy," Ariel replied. "Sharks don't glow. Come on!" Ariel and Flounder kept swimming.

When they swam closer, they saw the lights weren't one big creature, but a school of fish! Each fish was covered in glowing blue spots, and they circled above the night lilies.

One of the fish saw Ariel and Flounder. "Can you help us?" it cried.

"Are you going to make us follow you, and we'll be lost forever?" Flounder asked.

"Of course not! We're the ones who are lost!" the fish replied. "We're glowing toadfish. We belong near the shore. We've tried and tried to find our way back, but we always end up by these flowers."

“I know how to help!” Ariel said. “Follow me!” Ariel, Flounder, and the school of fish swam up and up. Soon their heads broke the surface.

“From far away, the night lilies look like you,” Ariel explained. “That’s why you keep swimming toward them.” She pointed up to the night sky. “Just follow that bright star instead! You’ll find the shore.”

The fish spun around and around Ariel in thanks. Then they swam off. Ariel and Flounder dove down to the night lily field. They picked as many flowers as they could carry.

A few minutes later, the border guards saw what looked like two bright blue eyes racing out of the darkness at them.

"It's the ghost lights!" they yelled.

"Don't worry! It's just me and Flounder," called Ariel. The guards laughed in relief.

"Princess," said one guard, "you shouldn't be out past the border in the dark."

"I'm not afraid of the dark—or ghost stories," replied Ariel. "Plus, my sister needs this medicine." Ariel and Flounder rushed to the palace with the glowing flowers.

The next morning, Andrina felt so much better that she couldn't stop talking—about how brave Ariel was!

A Winning Friendship

One sunny morning, Merida leapt out of bed and threw back the drapes. It was the perfect day for The DunBroch Games, a festival held in the spirit of fun and friendship.

Looking out the window, she saw clans arriving from across the kingdom. Merida could hardly wait to join the festivities—but first she had chores to do.

Walking out into the sunshine, Merida saw her parents, King Fergus and Queen Elinor. Standing between them was a boy.

"I want you to meet Kendrew," King Fergus said to Merida. "His father is a dear friend from a neighboring clan. I thought you could show him around."

Merida was thrilled. Now she could enjoy the games with someone her own age.

From the festival grounds, Merida heard the sound of cheering. “C’mon, Kendrew,” she said. “The games are beginning!”

The cheers grew louder as the bagpipers and drummers signaled the start of the games.

Waving goodbye to her parents, Merida dragged Kendrew away.

Queen Elinor watched them go. "I hope they get along."

But King Fergus wasn't worried. "I'm sure it will be a winning friendship, my love. Now, which way was the caber toss?"

Merida knew where she wanted to go first—the archery field! Surely Kendrew would like to shoot a few arrows.

Kendrew nervously watched as Merida hit bull's-eye after bull's-eye. When it was his turn, Kendrew confessed, "I don't have a bow."

“Here,” Merida said. “You can borrow mine.”

Kendrew smiled at her kindness and reluctantly took the bow. But he wasn’t the archer Merida was. In fact, he wasn’t much of an archer at all. His arrows hit everything but the target. Every time he missed, his expression grew sadder.

“That’s okay,” Merida assured Kendrew. But she felt bad. She had just wanted to find something for them to do together. Then she had an idea. “What kind of events do you like?”

Instantly, Kendrew perked up. “C’mon, I’ll show you!”

Kendrew led Merida toward a group of pipers. Scooping a set of bagpipes into his arms, he began playing.

Merida was confused. “But how do you win at bagpipes?” she asked.

“You don’t,” Kendrew replied. “You just play.”

"Here, you try!" Kendrew said, and passed the instrument to Merida.

Holding bagpipes reminded Merida of wrestling her brothers on bath day.

And when she tried to play a tune . . . what a ruckus! Kendrew saw that Merida wasn't having any fun. Now *he* felt bad. "Let's go find something else to do," he suggested.

Merida and Kendrew continued to wander through the fairgrounds, but neither was having much fun. It seemed like whatever she liked, he didn't.

And whatever he enjoyed, she didn't.

Merida wondered if there was anything she and Kendrew could enjoy . . . together.

Just then, they came to the last tent at the festival. They stopped in front of a sign that read "Pet Costume Contest."

Kendrew sighed. "I've always wanted to enter the contest. I love to sew, but I don't have a pet to make a costume for."

Suddenly, Merida had an idea.

Merida told Kendrew to wait for her at the tent and hurried off. When she returned, Merida wasn't alone. She had brought Angus!

"He's perfect!" Kendrew exclaimed.

Merida was happy. Maybe this was something they could do together. They were both excited to make Angus a new costume and win the contest!

Together they set to work.

While Merida schemed, Kendrew sewed.

While
Kendrew cut,
Merida calmed.

While Merida
wiggled, Kendrew
wobbled.

Working as a team, they had created an outfit never before seen (or worn) by man or beast.

When the contest ended, Merida and Kendrew had taken first prize!

"You were right, dear," said Queen Elinor, watching as the new friends rode off on Angus. "It was a winning friendship after all!"

Disney

Beauty and the Beast

The Bedtime Story

The sun was setting over the Beast's castle. Outside, the world was snowy and cold. But inside, Belle felt quite cozy. She had spent the past few days outside, taking her horse, Philippe, on strolls and even having snowball fights with the Beast.

Belle watched through her window as the Beast walked Philippe to the stables. Pausing, he gave the horse an awkward—but kind—pat with his large paw.

Suddenly, Chip bounced in. "Belle! Belle!" he called. "It's story time!"

"Now, now, Chip," Mrs. Potts said, coming in behind her son. "You must wait for Belle to offer to read you a story. Perhaps she is tired and wishes to go to bed."

"I'm all right," Belle replied, smiling. She'd gotten into the habit of reading bedtime stories with her new friends, and she'd been looking forward to it all day. "Let's go down to the library."

"Yippee!" Chip cried as he bounced out of the room.

Lumiere and Cogsworth were already in the library when the trio arrived. The pair had pulled Belle's favorite chair close to the crackling fire. A warm blanket rested over the back, and a thick book with a worn leather cover sat on the seat.

"I thought perhaps we could read this one tonight," Cogsworth suggested, pointing at the book.

Lumiere peered at the cover. *"Helmets Through the Ages: A Detailed History of Headwear,"* he read aloud. "Ahh, no! There must be some excitement! Some drama! Perhaps *l'amour*!"

"Let's read an adventure story! One with big, scary monsters!" Chip exclaimed.

"Nothing too scary, love," Mrs. Potts said gently. "You don't want to have nightmares."

Belle thought for a moment, her eyes skimming the colorful spines that lined the walls around them. Everyone wanted to read something so *different*. How would she find a story to make everyone happy?

Then Belle had an idea. "Why don't we make up our own bedtime story tonight?" she suggested.

"Our *own* story?" Chip asked, excited.

"Yes." Belle clapped her hands. "We'll go around in a circle and each add a line or two. It'll be fun!"

"A marvelous idea, dear," Mrs. Potts said.

"Magnifique!" Lumiere agreed.

"Quite!" Cogsworth added.

So the friends gathered around the fire, eager to begin.

Everyone insisted that Belle go first.

“Okay,” she agreed. She thought for a moment and then began. “Once upon a time, there was a knight named Sir Allard. Sir Allard was noble and brave. Wherever he went, he rode upon his trusty steed.” She smiled, thinking of Philippe.

“Did they fight dragons?” Chip shouted, bouncing eagerly.

Belle laughed at the teacup. “Why don’t you go next and tell us?”

"Sir Allard went on lots of adventures. He fought big, scary dragons and saved lots of princesses," Chip said. "People came to his castle from all over to ask for his help."

"Ooh, I believe I have something to add," Cogsworth said.

"Wonderful!" Belle said encouragingly.

"Sir Allard's castle was of the concentric variety. A vast improvement on the motte and bailey castle, the concentric design was a combination of the shell keep and the rectangular keep. It had many lines of defense in the form of multiple stone walls. The stone that was used was particularly interesting. . . ."

Cogsworth paused as he noticed Lumiere gesturing for him to finish his part.

"Well, yes, I suppose that was a few lines," Cogsworth sputtered.

"You gave us great details about the setting," Belle said kindly. "Lumiere, would you like to continue?"

"But of course," the candelabrum said. "One day, our hero, Sir Allard, heard about a ferocious dragon. As all brave knights know, where there is a dragon, there is often a princess. And so, dreaming of rescuing the princess and finding true love, Sir Allard set off to find the dragon. He soon found himself in an enchanted forest—a forest that was so dreadfully dark that he could not see!"

"Ooh!" Mrs. Potts exclaimed. "I know what happens next!

“As Sir Allard’s eyes adjusted, he saw something large resting in the distance,” Mrs. Potts said. “It appeared to be the dragon, but the creature didn’t look like the knight thought it would. In fact, it looked a bit sad.”

“What did he do, Mama?” Chip asked.

“Well, now, I’ve had my turn, Chip,” Mrs. Potts said.

“We’ve all had our turns!” Cogsworth exclaimed. “Who will finish the tale?”

Suddenly, a cough came from just outside the library door. The group turned to see the Beast standing in the doorway. He had been listening to their story the whole time.

"Hello," Belle called. "Would you care to come in and help us finish the story?"

"No," the Beast said gruffly, turning to leave. "I wouldn't know what to say. . . ."

"Ah, you can do it," Lumiere said.

"It's easy!" Chip added.

"Please," Belle said, motioning for him to pull up a chair.

"All right." The Beast strode over and sat next to Belle. "Well, I thought that . . . maybe . . . I don't know. This is ridiculous," he said, fidgeting nervously.

Belle put her hand on his paw and smiled encouragingly. He looked at it and then tried again. "The knight saw that the dragon was upset . . . and . . . lonely . . . so Sir Allard talked to him. And something very unlikely happened: the two of them became, well . . . friends. The end."

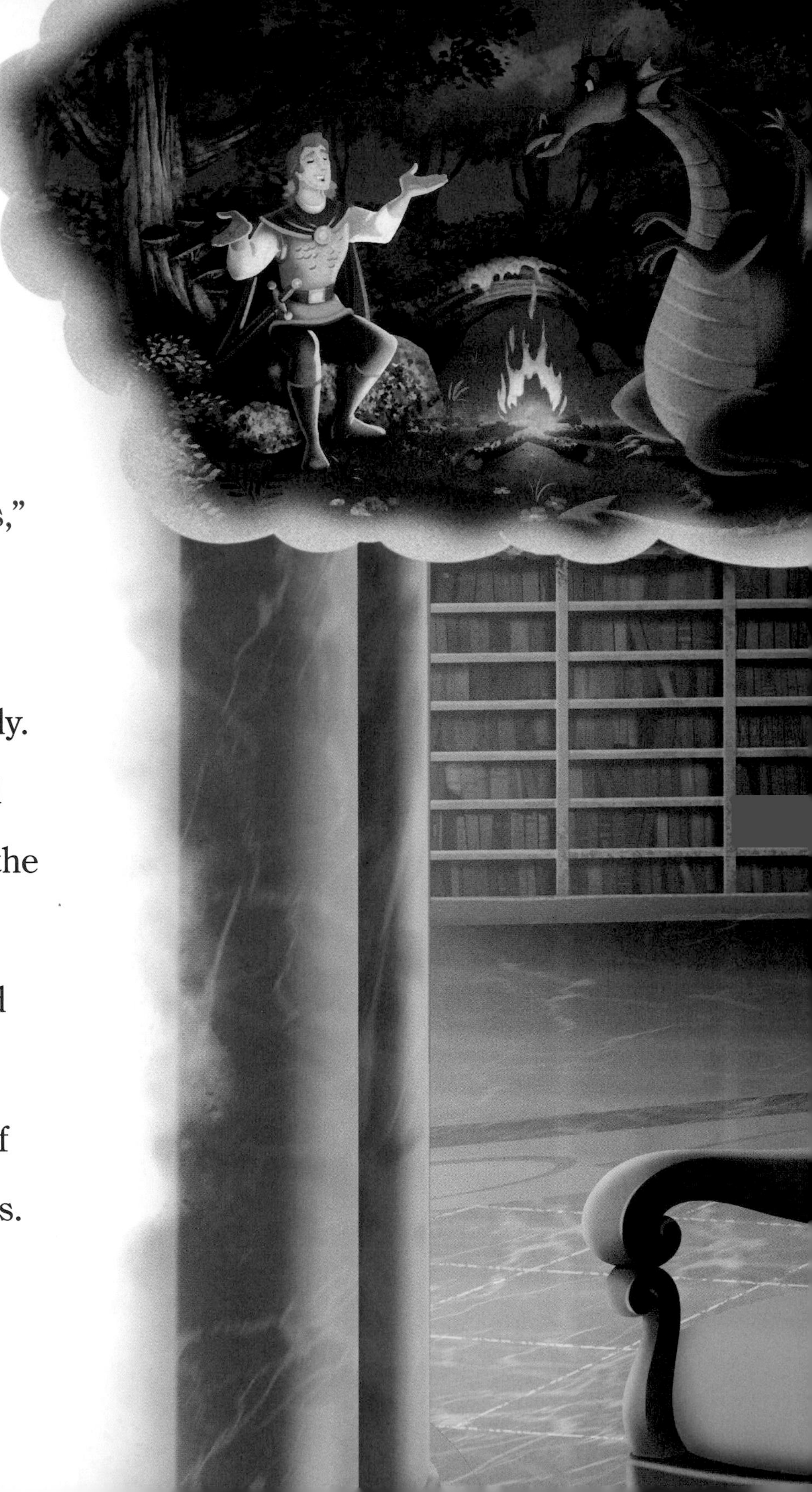

The room was quiet for a moment. Then everyone began to speak at once.

"Tres bien!" Lumiere exclaimed.

"Splendid, sir!" Cogsworth cried.

"Very well done, indeed," Mrs. Potts said.

"Yes," Belle said, "that was a wonderful bedtime story"—she smiled at the Beast, who seemed to keep surprising her—"with the most perfect ending."

Toy Story of Terror!

It was a dark and spooky night. A woman was being chased through a cemetery by a vampire. The vampire was getting closer . . . and closer. Suddenly, someone screamed.

"Run, Betsy, run!" Rex called out.

Bonnie and her family were in the car, on their way to a family vacation. Bonnie's toys were in the trunk of the car, watching a scary movie.

"Bor-ing," Mr. Potato Head grumbled.

"Patience," Mr. Pricklepants advised. "All great horror films start slowly."

Mr. Pricklepants was an expert on scary movies. In fact, he considered himself an expert on *all* movies. And plays. And books . . .

Inside the car, Bonnie rubbed her eyes. “Are we there yet?” she asked with a yawn.

“Not for a few more hours,” her mom replied. “You can go back to sleep.”

Ka-thump! Just then, the car hit a pothole and blew a tire.

The toys went flying. Jessie fell into a toolbox and the lid slammed shut. “Help!” she screamed.

Woody and Buzz Lightyear jumped into action. The two forced open the box and helped Jessie climb out.

Jessie was shaken. "I couldn't . . . I couldn't find a way out," she said, gasping.

"What's the matter with Jessie?" Trixie whispered.

"She was abandoned in a box for years," Mr. Potato Head explained.

Outside, thunder boomed and lightning flashed. The storm was getting worse.

Bonnie's mom pulled over at a roadside motel. The family would be staying there until the tire on their car was fixed. Bonnie reached into the trunk and grabbed her toys.

"A roadside motel is one of the most common locales for a horror film," Mr. Pricklepants pointed out when they reached their room.

Mr. Potato Head decided to go look around.

"I wouldn't go out there if I were you," Mr. Pricklepants warned. "The first to leave usually gets it."

Mr. Potato Head scoffed. He wasn't worried.

The toys went after Mr. Potato Head, but he had vanished!

"Maybe this place is haunted," Mr. Pricklepants whispered.

The toys split up to look for Mr. Potato Head. Suddenly, Rex screamed! "Ewww! I stepped in something," he said, trying to wipe goo off his foot.

As Buzz looked around, he realized that Mr. Potato Head had stepped in the same stuff. He had left a trail of footprints!

Trixie followed the tracks to an air vent. As she looked down, she fell in and disappeared!

The toys followed Trixie into the vent, with Buzz's glow-in-the-dark features lighting the way.

"What happens now?" Rex asked Mr. Pricklepants.

"This would be the part where the characters get separated and then picked off one by one," answered the hedgehog.

Seconds later, something snatched Mr. Pricklepants! Then it snatched Rex! Woody, Jessie, and Buzz looked at each other and ran.

Just then, something slowly crept out of the darkness toward them. It was Mr. Potato Head's arm!

"It's trying to tell us something," Buzz said.

"It's the number one," Woody said.

"I think, maybe, it's pointing up," Jessie said.

Above the toys was a vent. The trio followed it to a bathroom.

As Jessie looked around, something snatched Woody and Buzz! Then something pulled Jessie under the sink. It was Combat Carl, a soldier toy with a missing hand. "This place isn't safe for toys," he warned her.

The pair heard a noise. "We're trapped!" Jessie cried.

"Combat Carl never gives up," the soldier toy said. "Combat Carl finds a way."

The toys tried to run, but something snatched Combat Carl. Jessie was on her own.

The cowgirl hid in the bathtub. Seconds later, she heard a loud *RRRIP!* Claws slashed at the shower curtain! As Jessie backed up, an iguana appeared. It had Mr. Potato Head's arm in its mouth!

Jessie prepared for the worst, but the iguana was actually friendly. It swallowed the arm in one gulp and then gave Jessie a big lick. Grabbing her gently in its mouth, the iguana carried the cowgirl to a room behind the motel's lobby. He set her in a basket and rang a bell. *Ding!*

"Excellent find, Mr. Jones," the manager said, coming into the back room. He had trained his pet iguana to steal toys from motel guests so he could sell them on the Internet.

The manager posted Jessie's picture on a website and put her in a glass cabinet. The cowgirl's friends were there, too—even Combat Carl and his friend Combat Carl Junior.

A few minutes later, the manager returned. He checked his computer. He had sold Woody!

Reaching into the cabinet, he grabbed the cowboy and packed him in a box. A delivery truck would be arriving soon to pick up the package.

"Woody," Jessie whispered sadly.

"What started out as a classic horror film has turned into something more of a tragedy," Mr. Pricklepants observed.

A few minutes later, the manager sold Jessie, too. He had just taken her out when the mechanic arrived to fix Bonnie's family's tire. The manager put Jessie down and went to speak with the mechanic.

Jessie tried to unlock the cabinet, but she couldn't reach the latch. Even worse, the delivery truck had arrived. The driver came into the back room and took the package with Woody inside!

Jessie didn't know what to do, but Combat Carl had a plan.

"Listen," he said, "in a few minutes, the delivery lady is going to come through that door and take the other boxes, and you're going to be in one of them."

Jessie panicked. “I can’t get in a box!” she said.

“Jessie!” the soldier shouted. “When Combat Carl gets stuck in a jam, he says to himself, ‘Combat Carl never gives up. Combat Carl finds a way.’ Now say it!” he ordered.

Jessie tried. “Combat Carl never gives up. Combat Carl—”

“You’re not Combat Carl!” he shouted at her.

“Oh. Jessie never gives up. Jessie finds a way!” the cowgirl declared, finally understanding.

Jessie snuck into the empty lobby. Opening one of the boxes the manager had packed, she freed a robot toy. Bravely, Jessie crawled into the box in the robot's place. If she could get on the delivery truck, she could free Woody.

The plan was working—until the delivery lady taped the box shut and threw it in the truck!

Jessie began to panic. Then she remembered Combat Carl's words. "Jessie never gives up. Jessie finds a way," she told herself.

Feeling around, the cowgirl found a paper clip. She used it to slit the tape and crawled out of the box. Then Jessie found Woody. The two returned to the back room to free their friends!

Suddenly, Jessie heard Bonnie's voice coming from the lobby. The tire was fixed. Bonnie's family was getting ready to leave!

The cowgirl raced toward the curtain that separated the back room from the lobby. She was almost there when Mr. Jones caught her. Jessie kicked the iguana, and he spit something out.

"My hand!" Combat Carl shouted from inside the cabinet.

Mr. Potato Head's arm was also inside the iguana's mouth. Jessie grabbed the arm and used it to pull the curtain open.

At that moment, Bonnie looked through the curtain and saw the cabinet. “My toys!” she cried, running into the back room.

“Are those my daughter’s toys?” Bonnie’s mom asked the nervous motel manager.

Meanwhile, Mr. Jones put Jessie in the basket on the floor and rang the bell.

Looking down, Bonnie saw the cowgirl. “Jessie!” the little girl shouted, pointing at her doll.

Later, back in the trunk of Bonnie's family's car, the toys celebrated. "You did it, Jessie. You saved us all," Buzz said.

"Jessie didn't give up. Jessie found a way," the cowgirl said.

Mr. Potato Head looked fondly at his arm. "We ain't never gonna get separated again," he said.

Ka-thump! Just then, the car hit a bump and Mr. Potato Head's parts scattered around the trunk. "Aw, nuts," he said.

Everyone laughed—and that, Mr. Pricklepants noted, was a sure sign the story had reached its end.

Disney

THE LION KING

Who's Responsible?

Simba was far from home when he met Timon and Pumbaa.

"You okay, kid?" Timon asked.

"I guess so," Simba said with a sigh. Timon and Pumbaa could tell the lion cub was lost, tired, and sad. They invited Simba to join them.

Timon and Pumbaa liked the easy life—no problems, no responsibilities. And they had a motto that summed up their attitude.

“Repeat after me,” Timon said. *“Hakuna matata.”*

“It means ‘no worries,’” Pumbaa explained. When his new friends took him to their jungle home, Simba was amazed by its beauty.

“You live here?” he asked, impressed.

"We live wherever we want," Timon said.

Simba liked his new friends' carefree way of living. They didn't care about where he was from or why he'd run away. And that was just fine with Simba.

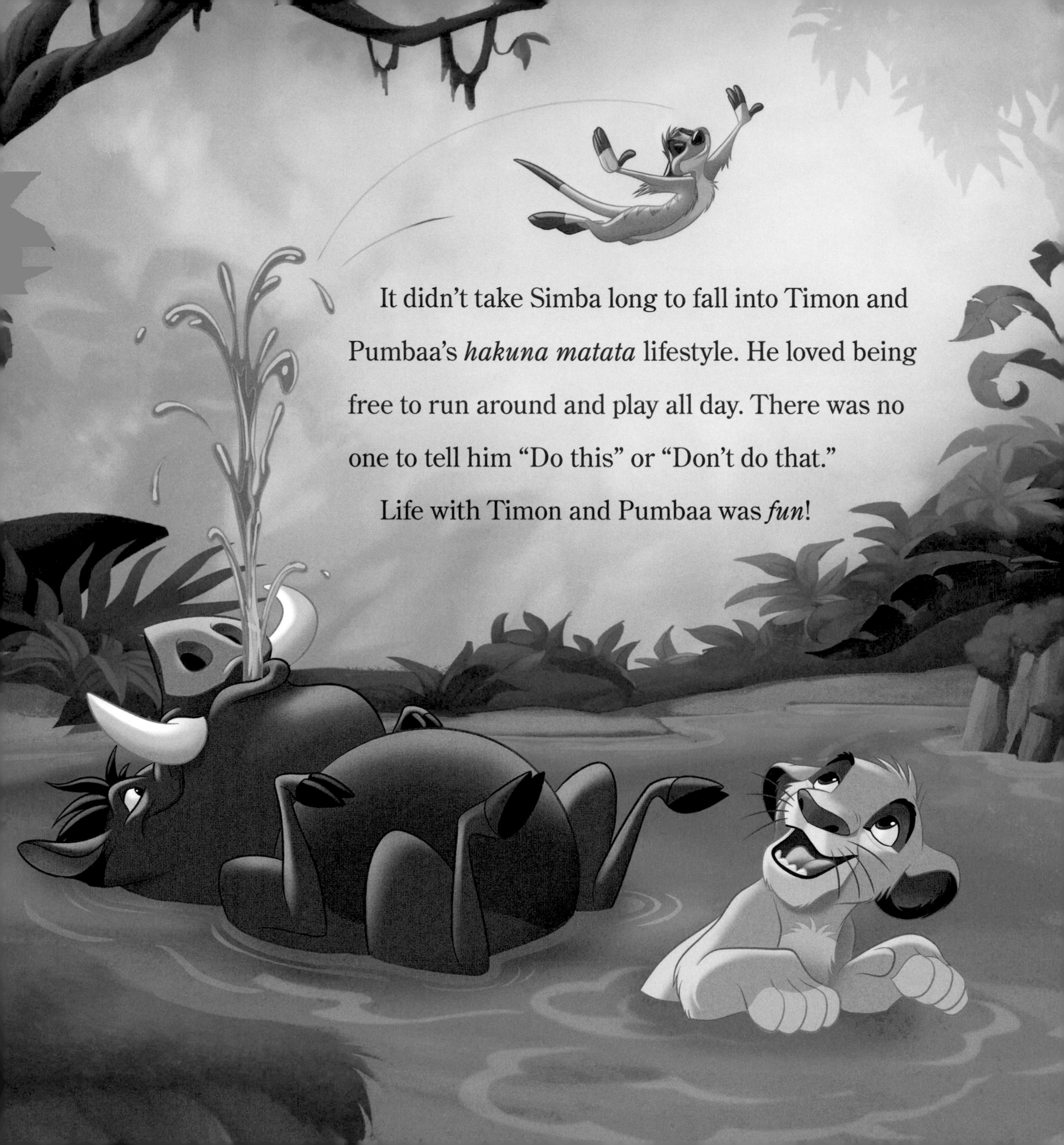

It didn't take Simba long to fall into Timon and Pumbaa's *hakuna matata* lifestyle. He loved being free to run around and play all day. There was no one to tell him "Do this" or "Don't do that."

Life with Timon and Pumbaa was *fun*!

When Simba and his new friends came across a big mud puddle, Simba was the first to jump in.

"This is great!" he shouted. He could get as muddy as he wanted and didn't have to take a bath. No worries!

Pumbaa jumped in, too, splattering mud everywhere.

"Whoa, nice one, Pumbaa," Timon said, laughing.

After a full day of playing in the mud, eating bugs, and living like Timon and Pumbaa, it was time for bed.

While Pumbaa slept, Simba and Timon stayed up, telling jokes and funny stories. Then Timon stood up and yawned.

"Well, that's it for me, kid," he said, climbing into his hammock. "I'm beat. Good night." Within moments, he was fast asleep.

Pumbaa and Timon snored loudly. Simba was having so much fun trying to catch fireflies, he didn't mind that his friends had fallen asleep.

Simba was too excited to go to bed. The jungle looked and sounded so different at night. It felt magical, and he wanted to be a part of it! Besides, he was sure he'd be fine in the morning no matter how late he stayed awake.

The sleepy cub chased fireflies and watched the moon and the stars. He had fun meeting animals who stayed awake at night and slept during the day. At last, he stumbled home and fell asleep.

The next morning Timon and Pumbaa tapped Simba on the shoulder to wake him up. The young lion groaned. Timon and Pumbaa wanted to go to the water hole, and Simba was grumpy. The water hole was a great place to meet friends. But all the other animals kept their distance from Simba.

“I hate to say this, kid, but you need a bath!” Timon blurted out.

“What do you mean?” asked Simba.

"I know a lot about this," Pumbaa said. "And the fact is, Simba, you stink."

"No way," Simba insisted. "I don't smell a thing."

"But we do, kid. Take a look," Timon said, pointing at the other animals. "No one is standing downwind."

Simba ran off, upset. *Hakuna matata* was supposed to mean no worries and no responsibilities. It wasn't supposed to be about when to take a bath or go to bed or eat dinner!

When they left the water hole, Simba seemed very sad. “I feel like I don’t fit in here,” he said.

“We understand about not fitting in,” said Pumbaa in a kind voice.

“Sorry, kid,” Timon added. “That’s not what we wanted to happen.”

“No, it’s not,” said Pumbaa. “Before you came here, somebody probably told you what to do all day long.”

“Now you gotta do that for yourself,” Timon continued.

Suddenly, Pumbaa had an idea. “Hey, we can help you learn about responsibility by being responsible ourselves!” It sounded good to Simba.

“Can we give it a try?” Simba asked. Timon looked at his friends and agreed.

Timon and Pumbaa took Simba to one of their favorite places for a bath. Simba splashed for a bit and then washed off the grime. “It does feel good to get all that dirt off me,” he admitted.

“You’ll smell better, too,” Timon said.

Pumbaa’s stomach rumbled. “And taking a bath makes you hungry!”

“Well, come on, then,” Timon said. “Let’s eat!”

The friends went to a place where several trees had fallen. Simba began trailing a plump beetle.

"Simba, I know you're still new at this," Timon began. "But we need lots of bugs, not just one."

"I know," Simba replied. "I'm just following a hunch."

"Pretty sure that's a beetle," joked Timon.

When the beetle scurried under a rotten log, Simba and Pumbaa worked together to break it open.

"Look at that," gasped Timon. "A big, beautiful buffet!"

After dinner, Timon made a bag out of a leaf. He explained, "I'm gonna save some bugs so we'll have something to snack on later."

"Great idea!" said Pumbaa. Working together to make sure there was enough food meant no one would go hungry.

Timon, Pumbaa, and Simba found a nice place to lie down and go to sleep for the night. Timon was fidgety and couldn't seem to get comfortable.

"I need some water," he said. Then, after lying back down, he said, "Ah, still thirsty."

After a few repeats of that, Pumbaa finally said, "Timon! Go. To. Bed."

"Okay, okay," Timon said. "But I'll never fall asleep if I'm still thirsty."

Moments after he lay down, however, Timon was snoring.

Simba smiled. If Timon can do it, I can do it, he thought. Then, he closed his eyes and drifted off to sleep.

He dreamed of the fun day he had with his friends and of all the adventures he would have with them tomorow. He slept well knowing he was happy living with his friends.

Over the next days, the friends realized something important. Working together, encouraging each other, and setting up routines really did make their lives better. Simba, Timon, and Pumbaa felt great.

The three friends lived their carefree way of life for a very long time. They still had their motto, but they added a little twist: living problem-free . . . responsibly! *Hakuna matata!*

Night-Lights

"I see one! I see one! Pull over, Mr. Fredricksen!" Russell said. Carl swerved the station wagon to the side of the road.

"Is it a squirrel?" asked Dug as he jumped out of the car.

"Even better!" said Russell. "According to the *Wilderness Explorer Guide to Flora and Fauna*, it's a Japanese morning glory."

They were headed to Sylvan State Park to earn Russell's Better Botanist Badge—his first as a Senior Wilderness Explorer. All he had to do was find and identify ten varieties of wildflower.

"Only nine more to go," he said as he took a photo of the flower.

"We'd better get moving then," Carl said.

As they drove, Russell looked at the flowers in his field guide.

"Wow, this book has everything in it," he said. "It has sunflowers. It has butterfly milkweed. It has purple wisteria."

"Does it have a ghost crocus?" asked Carl with a sly smile.

"A what?" asked Russell.

"A ghost crocus," said Carl. "It's a legendary flower that blooms only at night. Pale as the moon—glows in the dark—with six silver petals and stars on its stamens.

"Brave explorers have looked for it for centuries. Most people don't think it exists, but Ellie swore she saw one once—at the very park we're going to."

"Wow!" said Russell. Then he frowned. "I don't see it in the field guide."

"Like I said, most people don't think it exists," said Carl.

When they reached the park, it was already midmorning.

It took a while to find their campsite . . .

. . . and set up their tents. By the time they were ready to hike, it was midday.

They spent the day searching for flowers in Russell's guide. By the time the sun was setting, they had found ten varieties of wildflower! But Russell couldn't stop thinking about the ghost crocus.

"Please, Mr. Fredricksen," said Russell as they walked back to the campsite, "can we look for a ghost crocus?"

"Sorry," said Carl. "It's getting late. We have to get back to camp before dark."

That night, they sang around the campfire and told each other ghost stories.

And then they looked at the constellations.

"All right, it's getting very late. It's time for bed," Carl said, opening his tent. He had forgotten all about the ghost crocus.

But Russell hadn't. He couldn't sleep knowing there was another flower he could find and identify. Hiking at night might be dangerous for a *Junior* Wilderness Explorer, but Russell was a *Senior* Wilderness Explorer. He knew he could handle it!

"Let's go, Dug," he whispered. "We're gonna go fetch something."

"I *love* fetching," said Dug.

The woods were a lot darker than Russell had expected. Maybe Mr. Fredricksen was right. It was getting very late.

But then he spotted a soft glow. It seemed to be coming from the back of a cave. What he didn't see was the steep drop! Too late! He tumbled down into the mouth of the cave.

"Oh, no! Are you okay?" said Dug. Dug didn't hear a response from the cave, so he ran back to the campsite.

Carl awoke to a wet tongue licking his face.

"Master! Master! We were out in the dark looking for the ghost flower, and then he fell into the cave!"

"What?" cried Carl. "Quick! Lead me to him!"

Down in the cave, everything went dark. At first, Russell felt alone and afraid.

But then he remembered: he was a Senior Wilderness Explorer. "I can handle this!" he said to himself. He stood up and saw a glimmer of light. It was coming from around the corner.

“Russell!” someone cried. It was Carl. He had tied a rope to a tree and was lowering himself down into the cave.

“Look!” cried Dug happily. “I have fetched my master and brought him back!”

“I’m sorry, Russell,” said Carl. “I shouldn’t have told you that story about the ghost crocus. Honestly, I never believed it myself. Ellie always had a great imagination.”

“Well, I found something anyway,” said Russell with a sly smile.

“Well, I’ll be,” said Carl.

The next morning, Russell, Dug, and Carl packed up their things and headed back home.

"The Wilderness Explorers are going to be so excited I found all the wildflowers plus one!" Russell chattered away in the back seat.

"Thank you, Ellie," Carl whispered with a smile.

Disney

Pinocchio

A Real Boy

The sun was just beginning to rise over Pinocchio's little village. The moment he awoke, Pinocchio leapt out of bed and ran to look at himself in the mirror.

He laughed with joy when he saw his reflection. It hadn't been a dream. The Blue Fairy had made him a real boy!

He smelled a wonderful scent coming from the kitchen.

As he sniffed the air, Pinocchio felt a strange sensation: his mouth began to water. *Is this what being hungry feels like?* he wondered.

Pinocchio put on his clothes and ran to the kitchen. There he saw his father, Geppetto, cooking a huge breakfast. There were eggs, and pancakes, and bacon, and sausage, and oatmeal, and orange juice, and toast, and milk, and muffins, and . . . Pinocchio stopped trying to name everything on the table.

Geppetto grinned when he saw Pinocchio. “I wanted to cook you something special for your first breakfast, but I couldn’t decide what to make,” he said. “So I made everything!”

Pinocchio's stomach rumbled as he looked at all the food.

"Well, come on," Geppetto said. "Dig in!"

Pinocchio sat down and tried a bite of eggs. "It's chewy!" he said, his mouth full. "And soft. And . . . delicious!" Pinocchio tried a little bit of all the food Geppetto had made. Every bite tasted different from the last.

"This is wonderful," Pinocchio said. "Can we eat all day long?"

"Oh, no." Geppetto laughed. "We'll be much too busy for that. I have so much to show you."

"Can we take the food with us?" Pinocchio asked.

"That's an excellent idea," Geppetto said. "We'll have a picnic!"

Geppetto packed a lunch, and he and Pinocchio left to explore the village.

The first thing Pinocchio noticed was how brightly the sun shone. He blinked as he left the dark cottage and walked into the sunshine. Its dazzling beams felt warm against his skin.

Pinocchio and Geppetto made a game of running in and out of the shadows all the way to the edge of town. When Pinocchio jumped through the last shadow, he felt a strange sensation in his stomach. It was different from hunger. It was—

Hic. Pinocchio's tummy flip-flopped and a strange sound came from his throat.

"What—*hic*—is going—*hic*—on?" Pinocchio asked. He was starting to get scared.

"Don't worry," Geppetto said. "It's just the hiccups."

"Hiccups?" Pinocchio asked. "Will they ever—*hic*—stop?"

Geppetto showed Pinocchio how to hold his breath until the hiccups went away.

Pinocchio wasn't sure he liked this new experience. He had been so busy thinking about how much fun being a real boy was, he hadn't stopped to think about all the things that could go wrong.

Pinocchio grew silent as he followed Geppetto. At first, the sun's warmth had felt nice. But now Pinocchio was hot and sweaty. His feet hurt. And his stomach felt as empty as it had that morning before breakfast.

Pinocchio finally asked the question he was most concerned about: "Are we there yet?"

Geppetto took Pinocchio's hand. "It's just over this hill. . . ."

The pair climbed higher until they saw a beautiful valley below them.

"Race you to the swimming hole?" Geppetto asked.

Pinocchio nodded and ran off before Geppetto could get ready.

Father and son ran down the hill and collapsed in a happy pile next to the lake's edge.

"Time for food!" Pinocchio cheered.

Geppetto laughed and began unpacking the picnic basket.

Geppetto and Pinocchio spent the rest of the day at the swimming hole, playing in the water and fishing on the bank.

As they played, Geppetto told Pinocchio stories of the many times he had visited the lake as a young boy. Pinocchio felt much better now that he had eaten and rested. The cool water was refreshing after their long walk from the village. Even when Pinocchio scraped his knee on one of the willow trees, he didn't get upset. He was starting to realize what an exciting place the world was.

As the sun began to set, Pinocchio noticed a new feeling. His eyelids felt heavy, as though he could barely keep his eyes open. Then he yawned.

"I'm tired," Pinocchio said, surprised at the realization.

"You've had quite a big day," Geppetto said. "Are you ready to go home?"

Pinocchio nodded, and Geppetto lifted him onto his shoulders. He carried Pinocchio toward their little house in the village.

Sitting on Geppetto's back, Pinocchio looked up into the night sky. Far above them shone the Wishing Star, twinkling brightly. Pinocchio realized that being a real boy was more complicated than he had imagined.

“Today was fun, Father,” Pinocchio said. “But . . . it was hard, too.”

Geppetto nodded, thinking about what Pinocchio had said. “That’s what being alive is. It’s sunlight and bacon and hiccups and scraped knees. Some of it will be scary, but I promise I’ll be right there with you.”

Geppetto waited for Pinocchio to answer, but all he heard was the sound of soft snoring. Pinocchio was fast asleep!

Geppetto laughed. “Enough speeches. It’s time to get you to bed.”

Geppetto carried Pinocchio as gently as he could to bed. He fluffed his pillow and then drew the blankets close under Pinocchio's chin.

"Good night, my boy," Geppetto said, leaning in to kiss Pinocchio on the forehead. "Today was a dream come true. I cannot wait to share another adventure with you tomorrow."

A Royal Sleepover

"Psssst! Elsa?" Anna nudged her sleeping sister. "Come on, wake up."

Elsa shifted, groggy. "Go back to bed, Anna. It's the middle of the night," she said.

"I can't sleep!" Anna flopped down on Elsa's bed.

Then Anna smiled slyly to herself. She knew how to get Elsa out of bed. "Wanna have a sleepover?"

This time, Elsa opened her eyes and grinned. That sounded like a lot of fun!

While Anna went to her room to find extra pillows and blankets, Elsa headed to the kitchen to get the ingredients for her famous honey cones. After all, a sleepover wasn't a sleepover without snacks!

When Elsa got back to her room, she found Anna digging through the closet. She was looking for something.

"Aha!" Anna cried. "I knew it was here!"

Anna held up an old, worn book. Her parents had read it to the sisters every night when they were little.

"Let's see, we've got books, games, and this face cream Oaken gave me the last time I went to the trading post," Anna said. She opened the cream. "It looks kinda . . . goopy."

Elsa laughed. "Let's save that for later!"

Elsa looked around. It had been a long time since she'd had a sleepover. "Sooo . . . what should we do first?" she asked.

Anna was ready. "How about we build a fort, like when we were kids?" she suggested.

Anna stacked pillows and blankets around the room, making lookouts and hidden caves. Meanwhile, Elsa created icy tunnels and snowy turrets.

"This is fun," Elsa said, putting the finishing touches on an icy archway. "I think we should add a—"

SMACK! Elsa felt something soft and feathery hit her back. She turned to see a fallen pillow and a giggling Anna.

"Oh, no you don't!" Elsa yelled, launching a snowball at her sister. Anna ducked, squealing in delight.

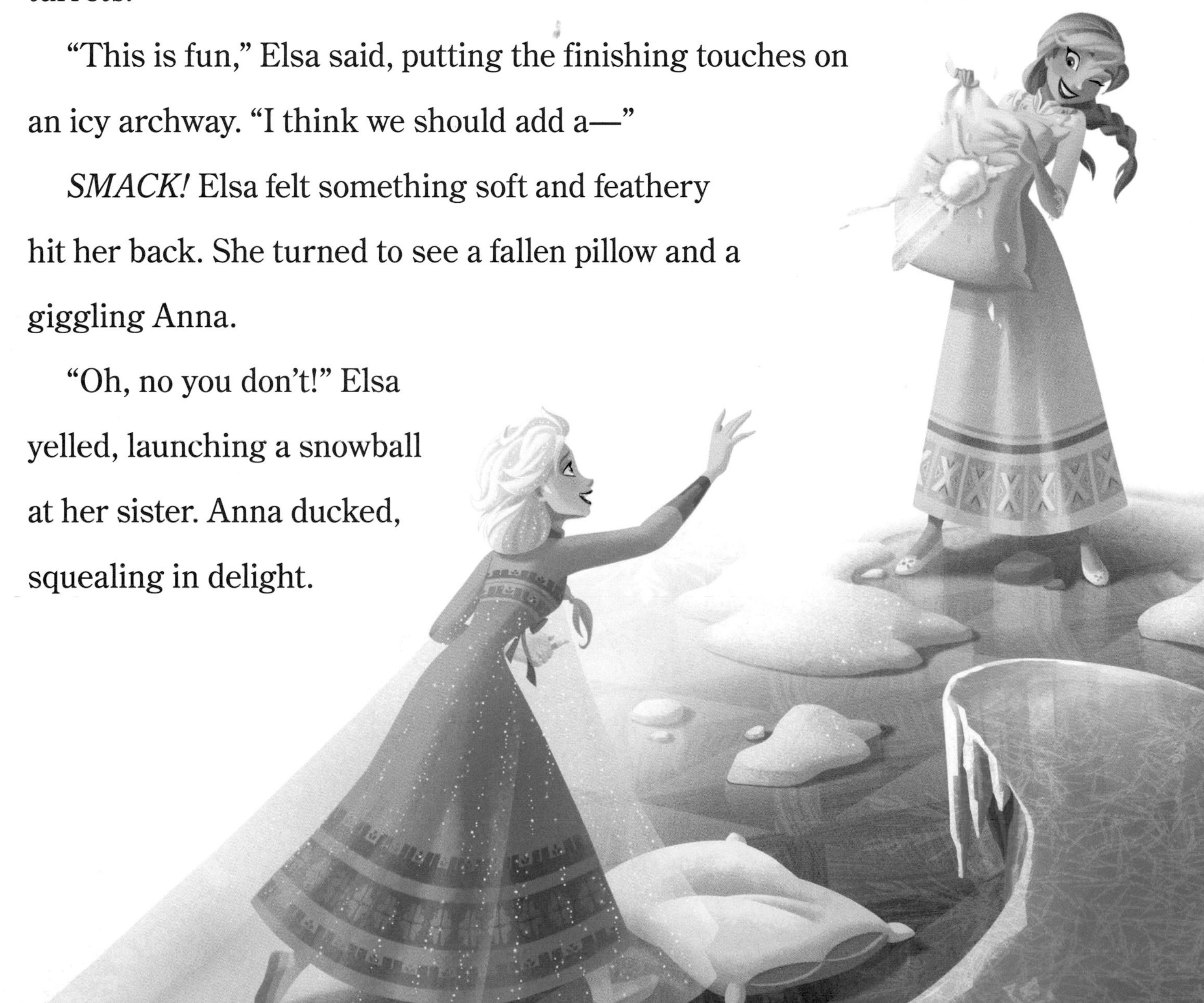

Olaf came to the castle to see what the sisters were up to. Elsa explained that they were having a sleepover and invited Olaf to join them.

"A sleepover?" Olaf asked, excited. "Oh, I've always wanted to have one of those." He paused. "What's a sleepover?"

"We'll show you," Anna said. "Come on! I bet you'll be great at Pick-Up Sticks!"

Anna was right. Olaf was a natural at the fun game.

Anna was great at Work of Art. She guessed the drawing and sculpture every time!

Charades proved to be a bit more challenging. Olaf twisted his body this way and that, making frantic gestures and grinning widely. The sisters didn't know what the answer could be. Finally, Elsa had an idea.

"Olaf, are you acting out 'summer'?" she asked.

"Yes!" he cried. "You're good at this!"

Elsa laughed. "Maybe it's time to do something else," she said. "How about a scary story?"

Anna went first, using her spookiest, most dramatic voice. She even held a candle up to her face, casting eerie shadows on the wall behind her. "According to legend, the Hairy Hooligan only comes out on nights like these, looking for his next victim," she said.

"How do you know when the Hairy Hooligan is around?" Olaf asked.

"He lets out a low moan," Anna answered.

"OOOOOOOHHHHH." A sad whine echoed through the room.

"Wow. That's really scary, Anna," Olaf said, impressed.

"Uh . . ." Anna blinked. "That wasn't me."

"OOOOOOOOOHHHHH!" The cry sounded like it was coming from outside the castle.

A sudden noise made them all jump. Elsa, Anna, and Olaf ran to the window. A shadowy figure was walking toward them!

"Stay here," Elsa said, running down the hall. But Anna and Olaf followed. They couldn't let Elsa face the Hairy Hooligan alone!

Elsa opened the castle door, and the friends peered into the darkness. Olaf held Anna's hand, bracing himself for the Hairy Hooligan's pointed teeth and sharp claws.

But it wasn't a monster after all. It was Sven!

"Sven!" Elsa called out. "What's the matter?"

Anna took one look at the reindeer and guessed what was going on. "You couldn't sleep, could you, Sven?" She patted him gently on the nose. "I bet Kristoff is snoring and keeping you awake. The trolls said his snores are loud enough to start an avalanche!"

Sven nodded.

"You should come to our sleepover!" Olaf said. "From what I can tell, there's very little sleeping involved."

Soon the group was happily settled in Elsa's room.

Anna got Sven and Olaf to try the face cream from Oaken, and they all laughed as the goop slid down their chins. "How about another story?" Elsa suggested, holding up a book.

"Excellent!" Anna agreed. She fluffed some pillows, and she, Olaf, and Sven got comfortable as Elsa began reading.

A little while later, Elsa finished the story. She looked up, hearing the sounds of heavy breathing around her. The rest of the slumber party had fallen asleep!

Smiling, Elsa put down the book. She gently tucked in Anna, Olaf, and Sven and climbed into bed. Then, with one last look at Anna and her friends, Elsa, too, drifted off to sleep.

Disney

Bambi

The Light-Up Night

The golden sun dipped behind the trees, bathing the forest in beautiful twilight. It was time for the animals to go to bed.

In the thicket, the little quails scurried one by one into their nest. The mice cuddled together in the thistles. Thumper and the other bunnies splashed each other as they washed up before bed. Bambi smiled as he curled up next to his mother.

One animal wasn't getting ready for bed, though. In the trees, Friend Owl was just beginning to wake up. He slept all through the day while the other animals were awake.

At night, when the moon rose into the sky, so did the wise old owl.

Friend Owl poked his head out of the hollow tree.

"Friend Owl! Tell us a bedtime story!" Thumper hollered. He was so excited that his foot went *thump-thump-thump*.

"Remember your manners," his mother said.

"Sorry," Thumper said. "Tell us a story *please*."

"Not tonight," Friend Owl said. "The shooting stars will soon put on a show, and I don't want to miss it!"

Bambi's ears perked up. What was a shooting star? He wasn't sure—but he wanted to find out. And Bambi wasn't the only one.

"I want to see the shooting stars, too!" Thumper cried.

"It's getting dark," Bambi's mother said in a soft voice. "And it's a long way to the meadow."

"I'll look after the young prince and Thumper," Friend Owl offered. "They'll be safe with me."

Friend Owl flew slowly overhead, watching as Bambi and Thumper pranced along beneath him. In the deepening darkness, Bambi and Thumper could hear the song of the crickets.

All of a sudden, Bambi saw a bright spark. "I saw it!" he cried.

Friend Owl smiled kindly at him. "No, Bambi," he said. "That was a firefly."

"Oh," Bambi said, watching in wonder as, one by one, fireflies lit up the meadow. It was a beautiful sight, but Bambi and Thumper still wanted to see the shooting stars.

The friends waited quietly as the sky grew darker. Soon there was just a thin sliver of moon gleaming overhead.

"That's good!" Friend Owl said approvingly. "A dark night will make the shooting stars easier to see."

Just then, a brilliant flash lit up the entire sky!

"Look!" Thumper shouted. "I saw the first shooting star!"

But before anyone could respond, a rumble of thunder rolled across the meadow. Thumper hadn't seen a shooting star after all. It was a bolt of lightning!

Bambi, Thumper, and Friend Owl scurried back to the forest as raindrops pelted the meadow. Thick clouds billowed across the sky, blocking the moon and stars. The friends huddled under the canopy of trees, waiting for the storm to pass.

Bambi sighed. With so many clouds covering the sky, how would he ever see a shooting star?

"I guess we'd better go home," Bambi said sadly.

Thumper was too disappointed to even thump his foot.

"Now, now, not so fast, little ones," Friend Owl said reassuringly. "Summer storms blow over before you know it. Be patient. The shooting stars are worth the wait!"

After a while, the steady drumming of the rain began to slow. A cool breeze ruffled the leaves—and blew the clouds from the sky.

"Is it over?" Bambi asked. "Can we see shooting stars now?"

"Let's find out," replied Friend Owl.

At the edge of the meadow, Bambi, Thumper, and Friend Owl saw that the fireflies had stopped flashing and the lightning was over. The night sky was clear but still.

Then it happened: a spark of light, high above them. It plunged toward the ground, leaving a shining white streak behind it!

Bambi gasped in surprise. “Was that it?” he asked. “A real shooting star?”

“That’s right, Young Prince!” Friend Owl hooted happily.

Soon another shooting star zoomed overhead, and another, and another! The night sky was full of them!

The three friends watched the sky for hours. Finally, there were no more stars.

“It’s time to go home now,” Friend Owl said.

“But I want to see more shooting stars!” Thumper whined.

“And you will,” Friend Owl promised. “When the time is right.”

Back in the thicket, Bambi snuggled close to his mother. As he told her all about the shooting stars, he closed his eyes. Behind his eyelids, he could still see the brilliant shooting stars. It had been the perfect night!

Mickey's Campout

Mickey Mouse and his friends were excited. It was time for their annual campout!

Everyone had an important job. Mickey packed the tents. Goofy learned how to build a fire. Minnie and Daisy made dinner. And Donald bought some new flashlights.

"Is everybody ready?" Mickey asked when they had packed up the car. "Let's go!"

Mickey drove up a mountain and through the woods. Finally, he parked the car next to a lake. “Here we are!” he said.

“Gosh, smell the fresh air!” Goofy said as he took a deep breath. “What should we do first?”

“Let’s set up our tents,” Mickey suggested.

"I've never put up a tent before," Minnie said.

"It's easy!" Mickey told her. "Just slip the tent poles into the pockets."

"Um, Mickey?" Daisy said. "Where are the poles?"

Mickey's eyes grew wide. "Oh, no!" he exclaimed. "I forgot them!"

"That's okay, Mickey," Goofy said. "We'll have just as much fun sleeping under the stars."

As the sun started to set, Daisy shivered. “It’s getting a little chilly,” she said.

“Maybe we should build a campfire,” Donald suggested.

“Sure!” Goofy replied. “Let’s go find some firewood.”

Mickey and his friends hiked into the forest to gather some firewood. When they had enough, Goofy showed them how to pile the sticks inside a circle of rocks.

"Stand back while I light the fire, everybody," Goofy said. Then he frowned. "Uh-oh. I forgot to bring the matches!"

"Don't worry, Goofy" Minnie said. "Our sleeping bags will keep us warm. Now, who's hungry? We have hot dogs, corn—"

"And s'mores for dessert!" added Daisy.

But Minnie and Daisy found a big surprise when they reached the picnic basket: the basket had tipped over and something had eaten all the food!

"No tents, no campfire, and no dinner," grumbled Donald. "At least we have flashlights!"

Click. Donald pushed the button on the flashlight, but it didn't shine.

Click. He tried again. Nothing happened.

"Aw, shucks!" Donald cried. "I remembered to buy flashlights—but I forgot to buy batteries!"

Suddenly, a flash of lightning lit up the sky.

"Maybe we should just go home," Minnie said. "We can't camp in the rain without tents."

"Or dinner," added Daisy.

"Or a campfire," Goofy chimed in.

"Or flashlights," Donald said.

Mickey agreed and the group rushed to the car.

No one spoke for the whole drive home. Mickey could tell that his friends were very disappointed.

As they walked into his house, Mickey had an idea. "I know!" he said. "Instead of having a campout, let's have a camp-in! We can camp right here in the living room."

"Oh, Mickey, what a great idea!" Minnie cried. "That sounds like so much fun!"

Mickey got the tent poles from the basement. Then he put up the tents while Goofy built a fire in the fireplace.

Meanwhile, Donald found some extra batteries. In the kitchen, Minnie and Daisy made an even better picnic for dinner.

Outside, the rain kept pouring down, but Mickey and his friends didn't mind. Their tents were strong and sturdy. The fire was warm and toasty. The flashlights shone brightly. And their picnic was delicious!

A Trusty Babysitter

It was a beautiful evening. Lady and Tramp were dressed up for dinner. It was their anniversary, and Tramp had made reservations at Tony's. He had booked the same table where they had dined on their very first date.

Lady was busy making sure their puppies—Scooter, Fluffy, Ruffy, and Scamp—were fed, bathed, and ready to be tucked into bed. "Now, be good for your babysitter," she said.

"We will, Mama," Ruffy, Fluffy, and Scooter replied.

"You too, Scamp," Tramp said, eyeing his son.

Just then, a knock sounded at the dog door.

"Uncle Trusty!" barked the puppies. Wagging their tails, they pounced on him affectionately and licked his floor-sweeping ears.

"*You're* our babysitter?" Scamp asked.

"I am, indeed," Trusty replied.

"Don't let him give you any trouble," Tramp said.

"Trouble? Why, this little young'un wouldn't dream of giving Uncle Trusty any *trouble*," said the old dog. "Would you, Scamp?"

Lady and Tramp kissed their puppies good night and headed toward the dog door.

"Don't let the puppies stay up too late," Lady told her old friend. "One bedtime story and then it's straight to bed."

"Oh, don't you worry, Miss Lady," Trusty said. "If my grandpappy taught me anything, it's how to put a dog to bed! I'll have 'em snoring away like an old sawmill in no time."

Trusty followed the puppies to the parlor and settled on a cozy cushion right next to their bed. "Now then . . . where was I . . . ?" he said.

"You were going to tell us a bedtime story," Scooter said.

"Oh, yes!" Trusty chuckled. "A bedtime story! Fine idea! Don't mind if I do! Let's see now. . . . How does it begin . . . ? Once upon a . . ."

"Time?" Fluffy suggested.

"No . . ." Uncle Trusty shook his head. "Or, wait. Maybe yes! That sounds familiar. Once upon a time . . ." he restarted. "Er . . . eh . . . where was I again?"

While Trusty tried to remember his story, Scooter, Fluffy, and Ruffy yawned and closed their eyes. Soon they were fast asleep.

Trusty smiled down at the pups. "Well, now, that wasn't so hard," he said. "I don't know why Lady went on so. I do declare, there's nothin' to puttin' pups to bed! Sweet dreams, little young'uns."

Trusty leaned over the puppies' basket to give each one a gentle peck. "Wait one doggone minute," he said as he came to the third and final furry forehead. "Weren't there four of you before . . . ?"

Scamp was gone!

"Which way did he go?" Trusty asked, turning around. He turned two more times, but Scamp still wasn't there. Trusty put his nose to the floor in search of Scamp's trail.

Unfortunately, Trusty's sense of smell had been gone for years. But that had never stopped him before, and it wasn't going to now!

Trusty sniffed and sniffed, following his nose . . . straight into the piano! "Oh, excuse me, ma'am," he said.

Slowly, Trusty made his way to the kitchen, which looked as if a storm had just blown through it. There were smashed eggs everywhere. Milk bottles lay empty, their contents forming puddles on the floor. Big sacks of flour had been torn apart!

"I'd say the pup's been here," Trusty said with a sigh.

Scamp wasn't there anymore, but he had left behind a trail of floury paw prints.

Trusty followed the prints into the living room. It looked even worse than the kitchen. Jim Dear's newspaper was in tatters, and his slippers were torn to shreds. Darling's knitting had been unraveled. Yarn crisscrossed the room like a giant spiderweb.

“Which way did he go?” Trusty said again. He followed the yarn around and around and around the room, until at last it led him back into the hall and to the doggy door.

“Scamp?” Trusty called, eyeing the holes dug all over the yard. “Scamp, you come on back in here, you hear me? Listen to Uncle Trusty, now.”

But if Scamp heard Trusty, he wasn't letting on.

Trusty was about to call Scamp again when he noticed a hole at the base of the wooden fence. His old heart began to thump loudly.

Trusty hurried over to the fence as fast as his stiff old legs would allow. "Doggone it! The pup's gone and flown the coop!" he moaned. What was he going to do?

Trusty poked his head through the hole and then quickly pulled it back. He had seen Lady and Tramp strolling down the street toward home.

Poor Trusty! His beloved Lady had left her dear little puppies in his care and protection, and he had let her son run away.

Trusty plodded back into the house and sat by the doggy door to meet the couple and break the bad news to them.

"Trusty!" Tramp said, beaming, as he and Lady stepped through the door. "How did it go?"

Before Trusty could answer, Lady pranced up and kissed his cheek. "Dear Trusty. We really can't thank you enough. Let us go peek in on the puppies, shall we? Then you can tell us how everything went!"

Trusty hung his head and followed Lady into the parlor, dreading the story he had to tell. How was he going to explain that he had lost Scamp?

Suddenly, Lady turned around. “Trusty!” she said. “How ever did you do this?”

“Er, do what?” he said, confused.

Lady pointed to the puppies' basket. "Why, get Scamp to go to bed, of course. Even we have trouble making him settle down."

"Well, would you look at that," Tramp said, eyeing his son. "Well done, old chap. I'll tell you something: we'll definitely be asking you to babysit again!"